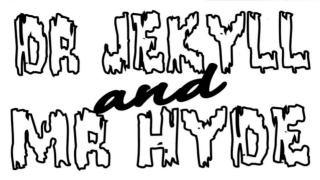

DR JEKYLL and MR HYDE

RETOLD BY PAULINE FRANCIS

EVANS BROTHERS LIMITED

First published in this edition in 2010
by Evans Brothers Limited
2A Portman Mansions
Chiltern Street
London W1 U 6NR

Cover design and illustration by Emil Dacanay, D.R. Ink
Inside illustrations by Gary Andrews

Printed in China by Midas Printing International Ltd.

British Library Cataloguing in Publication data
A cataloguing record for this book is available from the British Library.

ISBN 9780237541040

DR. JEKYLL and MR. HYDE

Introduction

Robert Louis Stevenson was born in 1850, in Edinburgh, Scotland. After studying law at Edinburgh University, he decided to earn his living as a writer. Unfortunately, he became ill with tuberculosis, a disease of the lungs, and he had to travel to warmer countries to improve his health. However, he did manage to earn some money by writing about his travels.

In 1880, Stevenson married Fanny Osborne, and, a year later, wrote *Treasure Island* for her young son. In 1886, *Kidnapped* was published. Both these books were popular but they did not make much money. So, in the same year, 1886, Stevenson wrote *The Strange Case of Dr Jekyll and Mr Hyde*. This was the story that made him well known and earned him more money because it was bought by adults.

Robert Louis Stevenson dreamed most of this story when he was ill and he wrote it down in only three days. It was Fanny who persuaded her husband to re-write it, changing it from a horror story into a serious story about good and evil.

The Strange Case of Dr Jekyll and Mr Hyde tells us that human beings have both good and evil in their nature. They struggle all the time to keep the evil away as well as fearing that this evil will dominate them in the end.

A year after this story was published, Stevenson's father died. With the money that was left to him, Robert Louis Stevenson and his family were able to live in Samoa, an island in the Pacific Ocean. The warm climate improved his health, and he lived and wrote there until his death in 1894.

CHAPTER ONE

Blackmail House

Mr Enfield shivered as he walked along the street. It was three o'clock on a black winter morning. Although the lamps were lit, he felt afraid and longed for the sight of a policeman.

"I've never seen these streets so empty," he thought.

Suddenly, the sound of running footsteps echoed in the street.

"Somebody is in a hurry," he muttered to himself.

A girl of about eight or nine came into Mr Enfield's view and he gave a sigh of relief. But at the same time, a small young man came rushing along the other street. He ran straight into the girl and knocked her to the ground.

Then the most terrible thing of all happened. The man trampled over the girl, as if he had not even seen her. She lay screaming on the ground – but the man ran on. He did not think about her at all. He did not seem human. Mr Enfield was too angry to be afraid.

"Come back here, sir!" he shouted.

But the man did not stop. Mr Enfield ran after him and dragged him back to the crying child.

"Look! Look what you have done!" he cried.

The man gave Mr Enfield a terrible look. By this

time, the girl's family, and a doctor, had arrived. Everybody took a great dislike to the man who had terrified the young girl; but he stood there, cool and calm with a sneer on his face. Mr Enfield stared at him.

"You must give this poor girl and her family some money," he told him. "You will pay up, sir, unless you want everybody to hear about this matter."

The man nodded and Mr Enfield saw that he was now very nervous because of the crowd.

"If you would like to come with me to my house," he said at last, "I shall find some money there."

Mr Enfield followed him to a clean, bright street. But two doors from the corner, the man stopped in front of a dirty building jutting out over the street. There was just a neglected door with peeling paint – no bell, no knocker, and no windows.

The man unlocked the door and went inside. A few minutes later, he came out with some coins and a cheque. Mr Enfield glanced at the name written on the cheque. He trembled.

"My God," he thought, "I know this name. He is a good friend of mine. How has he come to know such a terrible man as this? And why is my friend here in this wretched place? Perhaps this man is blackmailing him."

A few weeks later, Mr Enfield was taking a Sunday afternoon walk with his friend, Mr Utterson, a well-known lawyer. The two men found themselves walking down a narrow street, past a shabby doorway full of tramps. Mr Enfield stopped suddenly and pointed with his walking-cane.

"Do you see that door?" he asked.

"Yes," replied Mr Utterson. "It leads to an old laboratory at the back of Henry Jekyll's house."

"I didn't know that," said Mr Enfield. "I call it Blackmail House. Something strange happened here a few weeks ago. It was one of the most horrible things I have ever seen."

He told Mr Utterson about the man who had trampled on the child. His friend listened sadly and sighed from time to time.

"The man who signed the cheque, you say you know him well?" asked Mr Utterson. "Couldn't you have asked him about this place?"

"No," said Mr Enfield, "I didn't want to embarrass him. But I have studied this house a good deal since then. There is no other door. Few people ever go in and out of this one. There are three windows at the back, clean, but always shut. *Somebody* must live there. I have seen smoke coming out of the chimney."

"Do you know the name of the man who walked over the child?" asked Mr Utterson.

"Well, there's no harm in you knowing. He was called Hyde," said Mr Enfield.

Mr Utterson looked serious.

"Then I know the name of Hyde's friend, the man who signed the cheque that night," he sighed. "And now

I wish I hadn't heard your story."

"Perhaps I should not have told you," said Mr Enfield. "We'll say no more about it."

"Agreed," said the lawyer. "But just tell me one more thing. What does Hyde look like?"

There was a long silence.

"He's difficult to describe," said Mr Enfield at last. "There's something wrong about him. I do not know what it is. He seems deformed, but I could not tell you how. He looks strange."

Mr Enfield paused again and a shiver went through him.

"No, I can't describe him," he said, "although I can see him now in my mind. But I never saw a man I so disliked."

CHAPTER TWO

Hyde and Seek

Mr Utterson went straight home after his walk. Usually, after his Sunday meal in the evening, he sat by the fire and read until midnight. But tonight, he took a candle and went into his study. He opened his safe and took out an envelope. He took out some papers and read them.

> *The Last Will and Testament of*
> *Dr HENRY JEKYLL, M.D.*
>
> *"In the event of my death, all my possessions shall pass into the hands of my friend, Edward Hyde. In the event of the disappearance of Dr Jekyll beyond the period of three months, Edward Hyde shall step into Henry Jekyll's shoes."*

Mr Utterson put down the paper and sighed deeply.

"I thought this Will was madness then," he said to himself. "Now it is a disgrace. I must ask Lanyon what he thinks. I shall go there now."

Dr Lanyon was still dining when his friend arrived.

"Come in, come in," he said warmly. "Sit down."

"Lanyon," began the lawyer, "we're two of Henry

Jekyll's oldest friends, aren't we?"

"I suppose we are," laughed Lanyon, "but I wish we were younger friends!"

His face became serious again.

"I don't see much of him now."

"But you used to be good friends," said Mr Utterson. "You are both doctors – you have a lot in common."

"Yes," said Lanyon. "But about ten years ago, Jekyll began to go wrong. I mean, wrong in his mind. He became strange."

"Did you ever come across a young friend of his, a Mr Hyde?" asked the lawyer.

"Hyde?" repeated Lanyon. "No, I have never heard of him."

When Mr Utterson went back home and tried to sleep in his great dark bed, his mind was filled with strange images... a child falling and screaming, a man running away, a man with no face... and when he woke from this awful sleep, he had only one thought in his mind.

"I must see the face of Mr Hyde for myself," he thought. "Then I might understand why Jekyll has become his friend."

From that day, Mr Utterson began to haunt the shabby door of Blackmail House. Before work, in his lunch hour, and after work – he stood and watched.

"If he is Mr Hyde, then I shall be Mr Seek," he told himself grimly.

One day, his patience was rewarded. It was a fine, frosty night, about ten o'clock, when he first heard footsteps in the empty street. Mr Utterson held his breath. The footsteps came nearer. The lawyer peeped out from his doorway.

A small man was walking towards the door of Blackmail House. As he walked, he took a key from his pocket. Mr Utterson stepped out and touched him on the shoulder as he passed.

"Mr Hyde, I think?" he said.

Mr Hyde shrank away from him, afraid, and his breath hissed in the silent air. He did not look Mr Utterson in the eye.

"That is my name," he said. His voice was husky. "What do you want?"

"My name is Mr Utterson. I am an old friend of Dr Jekyll," said Mr Utterson. "You must have heard my name. May I come in with you?"

"You will not find Mr Jekyll here," said Mr Hyde.

He looked closely at Mr Utterson.

"How do you know me?" he asked suddenly.

Mr Utterson hesitated for a moment.

"May I see your face?" he asked.

Mr Hyde waited for a moment. Then he turned to Mr Utterson and looked at him full in the face.

"Now I shall know you again," the lawyer said quietly. "It may be useful."

"Yes, it is useful that we have met," Mr Hyde said. "And here is my address. That also may be useful in the future."

Utterson shivered. Was Hyde thinking about Jekyll's will?

"I repeat," said Mr Hyde, "how do you know me?"

"A friend described you to me," answered Mr Utterson, "a friend we both know."

"We do not have any friends in common," he said.

"I think we both know Dr Jekyll," said the lawyer.

Mr Hyde snorted with anger. Then he gave a terrible laugh.

"No! No! Dr Jekyll did not tell you!" he shouted. "You have lied!"

He put the key in the door. Utterson stared at the thick, hairy skin on Hyde's hand as he turned it. Then he stood for a moment after Hyde had gone inside, trembling with cold and fear.

'What is it about him?" he asked himself. "What is it?"

After a moment or two, he knew the answer to his own question.

"Yes, that's it," he thought. "The man hardly seems human."

CHAPTER THREE

Murder at midnight

About a year later, a man called Sir Danvers Carew was walking along a lane close to the River Thames. It was a cloudless October night with a full moon.

As he walked, he came face to face with a small man carrying a wooden walking-cane. Sir Danvers stopped and bowed and said:

"Good evening to you, sir."

The small man did not answer. His face became angry and he stamped his foot. Suddenly, he swung his walking-cane into the air. Sir Danvers took a step back in astonishment. This angered the small man even further. Without a word, he knocked Sir Danvers to the ground.

And the next moment, with ape-like fury, he was trampling his victim underfoot. He hit him over and over again, until Sir Danvers' bones cracked and his body jumped up and down on the ground.

Someone was watching this horrible crime – a maid living in a room above the lane. She was at her window, gazing up at the moon.

But when Sir Danvers' bones began to break, she fainted.

A few hours later, a policeman rang the bell hard at Mr Utterson's house. He had with him a letter addressed to the lawyer.

"Where did you get this?" asked the lawyer.

"It was found on the body of a murdered man, sir," explained the policeman.

The policeman told the lawyer about the murder in the lane.

"Good God!" said Mr Utterson. "Why would anyone do such a thing?"

"I don't know, sir, the poor old gentleman was only being polite. The maid is in a terrible state."

"Did she say anything else?"

"Yes," said the policeman.

He paused.

"She recognised the attacker. He used to visit her master once or twice a week."

"Who was he?"

"A Mr Hyde."

Mr Utterson felt himself tremble at the name.

The officer held out part of a walking-cane to the lawyer. Mr Utterson turned a ghostly white. There was no doubt now. *He* had given it to Henry Jekyll many years ago as a gift.

"Is this Mr Hyde small in height?" he asked in a trembling voice.

"Particularly small and particularly wicked-looking is what the maid said," answered the officer.

"Then I think I can take you to his house," said Mr Utterson.

They set off at once for the address that Hyde had given him. A thick, chocolate-coloured fog hung over London, the first of the season. The wind blew the fog through everywhere and the cab crawled from street to street. The light, such as it was, changed from moment to moment. As they came close to Hyde's house, the air was murky and the street muddy. To the lawyer's eyes, it seemed like a district of some city in a nightmare. His thoughts were as gloomy as the weather.

The cab turned into the dingy street. The fog lifted for a moment, revealing ragged children huddled in doorways, shabby women going out for a drink. Then, just as suddenly, the fog came down again. Now, hidden in a swirling dark fog, they stood outside the door of Dr Jekyll's friend.

A pale woman with silver hair opened the door. Her face was evil but she smiled at them.

"Is this the home of Mr Hyde?" asked the officer.

"Yes, sir, but he's not at home," she replied.

"When did you last see him?"

"He was here last night, very late. But he left soon after," the woman said.

"Does he usually do that?"

"Oh yes, sir," she smiled, "there's nothing strange in that. I hadn't seen him for two months until last night."

"We wish to see his rooms," said Mr Utterson.

"Impossible!" she replied.

"Then," said Mr Utterson carefully, "I had better tell you who this person is. This is Inspector Newcomen of Scotland Yard."

The woman seemed pleased by this. She flashed an evil smile at them.

"Ah!" she said, "he's in trouble! What has he done?"

"He don't seem a very popular character," said the Inspector. "And now, my good woman, just let me and this gentleman have a look at his rooms."

Mr Hyde used only two rooms in the house. They were well-furnished and there were good paintings hanging on the walls.

"No doubt these are gifts from Jekyll," thought Mr Utterson sourly.

There were clothes lying everywhere on the floor. Drawers were pulled open. In the fireplace was a pile of ash and half-burned papers, a cheque book. The Inspector looked around the room. Then he picked up the other half of a walking-cane. Mr Utterson looked at him in horror.

There could be no doubt – Hyde was a murderer.

CHAPTER FOUR

A murderer's autograph

"I must speak to Henry Jekyll at once," Mr Utterson muttered to himself. "He might be in danger. I must know what is going on."

He set off at once for his friend's house. When he arrived, Poole, the butler, led him through the garden to the laboratory that backed onto Blackmail House.

"I have never seen my friend in these rooms before," thought Mr Utterson.

He looked around him. The house had belonged to a famous surgeon, and here he had taught his students how to dissect bodies. Mr Utterson walked through the dimly lit room littered with boxes, up a flight of stairs and into his friend's study. Dr Jekyll did not get up to greet his friend. He only held out a cold hand and said "Welcome" in a strange voice.

"You have heard the news, Jekyll?" asked the lawyer.

Henry Jekyll shuddered.

"Yes," he whispered.

"Sir Carew was my client," said Mr Utterson, "but so are you. I want to know what is going on. You have not been mad enough to shelter this fellow, this Mr Hyde?"

"Utterson," cried the doctor, "I swear to God I will

never set eyes on him again. I give you my word of honour that I am finished with him in this world. He does not want my help. You do not know him as I do. He is safe, quite safe. He will never be heard of again."

The lawyer listened sadly. He was worried. The doctor seemed ill, feverish.

"I hope you are right, for your sake," he told the doctor. "If it came to a trial, your name might be mentioned."

"I am quite sure of Hyde," replied Jekyll. "But there is one other matter on which you can advise me."

He picked up an envelope.

"I have received this letter. Should I show it to the police? May I give it to you so that you can decide?"

Mr Utterson opened the envelope and took out the letter. He read it quickly.

"What was the postmark?" asked the lawyer.

"It was handed in."

"I'll keep it and think about it," said Mr Utterson.

"*You* decide," said the doctor, "I have lost all confidence in myself."

"Just one last word," said the lawyer. "Did Hyde tell you what to write in your Will?"

The doctor turned pale and looked as if he was going to faint. He clenched his lips tightly and nodded.

"I knew it!" exclaimed the lawyer. "He meant to murder you, not Sir Danvers. You have had a fine escape, Jekyll."

"I have had a lesson – O God, Utterson, what a lesson I have had!"

He covered his face with his hands..

Later, at home, Mr Utterson drank a glass of wine by his fire with Mr Guest, his head clerk. Fog still hung over the city; but his room was warm and bright.

"I do not keep secrets from Mr Guest," he thought. "And Guest has often been to Jekyll's house on business. He must have seen Hyde around the house. I shall show *him* Jekyll's letter. He may recognise the handwriting.

"This is a sad business about Sir Danvers," he said.

"Yes, sir, indeed," Guest replied. "There is much ill-feeling towards the murderer. The man is mad, of course."

"I should like to hear your views on that," said the lawyer. "I have a letter here in his handwriting. Do not speak to anybody about this. It is an ugly business."

He held out Edward Hyde's letter.

"Here it is," he said, "a murderer's autograph."

Guest looked at it carefully. "Not mad," he said, "but very odd." Just then, a servant came in with a note from Dr Jekyll.

"May I see the note?" asked Mr Guest.

"An invitation to dinner," replied the lawyer. "What interest is that to you?"

The clerk laid the two pieces of paper alongside each other. He studied them for a long time.

"They are very similar, sir," he said.

When Guest had left, Utterson locked the note in his safe. Then he cried out to himself, "Why is Henry Jekyll forging a murderer's signature?"

And as he spoke, the blood ran cold in his veins.

CHAPTER FIVE

Death of a friend

"What in God's name is wrong with Lanyon!" thought Mr Utterson. "He has the look of death written on his face!"

Utterson shuddered from head to toe as he looked at his friend. The doctor's rosy face was white and lined. His hair was thinner. But far worse was the look in Lanyon's eyes – a look of complete terror.

"What is wrong, dear friend?" cried Utterson. "You looked so well when I saw you at Jekyll's after Christmas. That was only two weeks ago! What has happened?"

"I have had a shock," the doctor replied, "and I shall never recover. I shall die soon. Well, life has been pleasant. I liked it, yes, sir, I liked my life."

"Jekyll is ill, too," said Utterson. "Have you seen him?"

Lanyon gave his friend a look of terror and held up a trembling hand.

"I wish to see or hear no more of Dr Jekyll," he said in a loud and shaking voice. "As far as I am concerned, that man is already dead."

"Oh dear," said the lawyer, "can I do anything to help? We are three very old friends and we shall not live long enough to make others."

"Nothing can be done," said Lanyon. "Ask Jekyll."

"He won't see me," said Utterson.

"I am not surprised at that," said Lanyon. "Some day, Utterson, after I am dead, you may perhaps learn the right and wrong of this. I cannot tell you. Now come and sit with me and talk of something else."

Later, when Utterson got home, he wrote to Dr Jekyll.

"...*Why will you not see me?*" he wrote...

"*What has caused this unhappy break with our dear friend, Lanyon?*"

A reply came the next day.

"*My dear Utterson*

I have quarrelled with Lanyon and there is nothing to be done about it. I do not blame him, but I share his view that we must never meet. From now on, I intend to stay at home alone. My door will be shut to you. You must not be surprised by this. You will still be my friend; but you must let me go my own dark way.

I have brought on myself a punishment and a danger that I cannot speak about. I did not believe this world could contain such terror for me.

You can do one thing to help, Utterson. You can respect my silence.

Your dear friend

Henry Jekyll"

27

Mr Utterson read the letter in amazement. Was his friend mad? But Lanyon had hinted at something darker and more terrible than madness. Lanyon knew – he must tell him what had happened.

But before Utterson could see him, Dr Lanyon took to his bed and died. He had left a letter for the lawyer, addressed by hand and sealed.

*"PRIVATE: for the hands of J.G. Utterson ALONE.
If he dies before me, to be destroyed unread"*

Utterson sighed and opened Lanyon's letter. Inside was another letter, also sealed and addressed in Lanyon's handwriting.

*"Not to be opened till the death or disappearance
of Dr Henry Jekyll."*

Utterson shivered. He had just returned from Lanyon's funeral, and now there was talk again of Dr Jekyll's disappearance. Mr Utterson locked the letters in his safe. The face of Mr Hyde came back to him. Something terrible was happening and he wanted to know what it was.

A few weeks later, the lawyer saw Dr Jekyll – but the sight chilled him to the bone.

CHAPTER SIX

A face at the window

It was a Sunday afternoon. Mr Utterson was taking his usual afternoon walk with Mr Enfield. They passed the door of Blackmail House.

"Well," said Enfield, "that story is at an end, at least. We shall never see Mr Hyde again."

"I hope not," said Utterson, "Did I ever tell you that I saw him, just the once? He repelled me, just as he did you."

"He repelled everyone," said Enfield.

Utterson stared up at the house, then walked towards the side entrance.

"Let's look at the windows at the back," he said. "I am very worried about poor Jekyll. I have paid him a visit many times since Lanyon's death. But the butler tells me the same thing every time. The doctor spends all his time in his study above the laboratory. He even sleeps there. He hardly speaks to the servants. He has something horrible on his mind, I know that."

They walked into the little courtyard. It was cool and damp there although the sun was still high in the sky. It felt as if night had come early.

"We might be able to cheer him up, even from here," said the lawyer.

They looked up at the windows. The middle one was half-open.

"Look, there is Jekyll!" cried Utterson, "sitting by the window! He looks like a prisoner."

Utterson went closer.

"Jekyll!" he shouted, "I hope you are feeling better?"

"I am very low in spirits," replied Jekyll in a tired voice, "very low. But it will not last long, thank God."

"You stay too much indoors, my good friend," said Utterson, "you should be walking outdoors, like us! This is Mr Enfield, by the way. Come on, Jekyll. Get your hat and take a quick walk with us."

Dr Jekyll gave a long sigh.

"You are very good," he said, "and I should like to go with you. But, no, no, no — it is impossible. I dare not. I am very glad to see you, Utterson, and your friend. I would ask you both up, but the place is untidy."

"Well, then, Jekyll, the best thing we can do is to talk to you from here," laughed Utterson, desperate to cheer up his friend.

Dr Jekyll smiled back.

"I was just going to suggest that…"

As he spoke, his smile disappeared. A look of complete terror came across his face. Enfield and Utterson watched him, and their blood froze at the sight of him.

At that moment, Jekyll shut the window.

But that glimpse of the doctor was enough. The friends walked away, pale and trembling. At last, Utterson broke the silence.

"God forgive us! God forgive us!" he muttered.

CHAPTER SEVEN

The last night

One evening in March, Mr Utterson was sitting by the fire and listening to the wind outside. The door bell rang and Dr Jekyll's butler, Poole, was shown into the room.

"Why, Poole!" said the lawyer in surprise, "what brings you here? Is the doctor ill?"

"There is something wrong, Mr Utterson," whispered the butler, "but I don't know what it is."

"Take this glass of wine. Sit down," said Utterson. "Now take your time and tell me what has happened."

"You know what the doctor is like," Poole began. "He shuts himself up in his room. Well, he's shut up again and I don't like it, sir." He hesitated. "I'm afraid, Mr Utterson."

"Now my good man," said the lawyer, "what are you afraid of?"

"I've been afraid for about a week," said Poole, "and I can bear it no more."

"Try and tell me what it is," said Utterson kindly.

"I think there has been foul play," said Poole.

"Foul play!" said the lawyer. He was suddenly afraid for Jekyll.

"What do you mean?"

"I daren't say anything, sir," said Poole, "but will you come along with me and see for yourself?"

Mr Utterson got up immediately, took his hat and overcoat and followed the butler. The wind was blowing harder outside. The moon was ghostly pale and tilted in the sky, as if the wind had blown it over. Poole rushed along the deserted streets, and the lawyer had to hurry to keep up with him.

"I wish there were more people about," thought Mr Utterson. "I feel I am going to see something terrible."

They reached the square where Henry Jekyll lived. The wind blew swirling dust into their eyes and almost snapped the thin trees in two. Poole stopped outside his master's house and mopped his forehead with a red handkerchief. His face was deadly white and he could hardly speak.

"Well, sir, here we are," he whispered. "And God grant there is nothing wrong."

"Amen, Poole," said the lawyer.

The butler knocked gently on the door.

"Is that you, Poole?" asked a frightened voice.

"It's all right," said Poole. "Open the door."

A fire burned brightly in the big hall. Around the hearth sat Jekyll's servants, huddled together like a flock of sheep. At the sight of the lawyer, the housemaid began to sob hysterically, and the cook ran forward crying.

"What are you all doing here?" asked the lawyer crossly. "You should all be at your work. Your master will not be pleased."

"They're all afraid," said Poole.

The silence in the hall was broken by the sound of a maid crying.

"Get me a candle," said Poole, "and we'll finish this business."

Mr Utterson followed Poole through the back garden, eerie in the light of the flickering candle.

"Come as quietly as you can," whispered Poole. "I want you to hear, and I don't want you to be heard. And," his voice could hardly be heard now above the wind, "if he asks you in, don't go."

Mr Utterson's nerve almost gave way when he heard this. He shivered violently. Then he gathered his courage and followed Poole into the dark laboratory, past crates and bottles, right to the foot of the stairs.

CHAPTER EIGHT

The return of Mr Hyde

"Wait here, sir," said Poole, putting down the candle. The butler crept up the dark staircase and knocked on the door.

"Mr Utterson is asking to see you, sir," he called.

"Tell him I cannot see anybody," said a hoarse voice.

"Thank you, sir," said Poole.

He came downstairs and led a surprised Mr Utterson back to the kitchen.

"Sir, was that my master's voice?" he asked.

The lawyer was very pale and worried.

"It certainly seems changed," he agreed.

"Changed? Changed?" shouted the butler. "I should think so! I have worked in his house for twenty years. I know my master's voice. Yes, sir. I know. My master's been murdered."

"Murdered?" cried the lawyer.

"Murdered!" answered Poole, "eight days ago. That's when I heard him cry out 'In the name of God!'. But who's there in his place?"

He stared at Utterson.

"Why does it stay there? Whatever is in there cries to God, Mr Utterson."

Mr Utterson sat in silence.

"This is rather a wild story, Poole," he said at last. "Suppose Dr Jekyll has been, well, murdered, why would the murderer stay? It doesn't make sense!"

"You are a hard man to convince, sir," said Poole, disappointed. "But I will convince you. Now, listen. All this week, Dr Jekyll – or whatever it is that lives in that room – has been calling out night and day for some medicine."

"Medicine?"

"Yes," said Poole. "He usually writes down his order for medicine and throws it down the stairs for me to collect. This last week has been terrible. Orders two or three times a day. Then he complains because the medicine wasn't right – 'not pure enough', he said."

Poole paused.

"Whatever he wants, he wants it badly," he finished.

"Are the orders in the doctor's handwriting?" asked Utterson.

"Yes," said Poole firmly.

Suddenly, his voice changed and he came nearer to the lawyer.

"In any case, I've seen him," he whispered.

"Seen him?" asked the lawyer. "How?"

"He was on his hands and knees," said Poole, "down in the laboratory. I think he was looking for medicine.

When I came in, he gave a strange cry and ran upstairs."

He looked closely at the lawyer.

"I only saw him for one minute, sir, just one minute. But the hair stood up on my neck. Oh, sir, if that was my master, why did he have a mask on his face? If it was my master, why did he cry out like a wild animal and run away from me? I have been his servant for a long time."

Poole stopped and put his hands over his face.

"Perhaps he is ill," said Mr Utterson kindly. "Perhaps he has had a stroke. It could have changed the look on his face. He thinks this medicine will cure him."

He touched Poole's arm.

"Do not be alarmed."

Poole's face was as white as snow.

"Sir," he whispered, "that thing was not my master. My master is a tall, strong man. This was more of a dwarf."

"No, it cannot be!" exclaimed the lawyer.

"Yes!" cried Poole, "do you not think I know my own master? No, that thing in the mask was never Dr Jekyll! God knows what it was, but it was never Dr Jekyll!"

Poole stared at Mr Utterson in the candlelight.

"I think my master has been murdered," he said.

"In that case, we shall go and see," said Mr Utterson firmly. "We shall break down the door."

They crossed the yard again together. Clouds hid the moon now. The wind was strong and almost blew out their candle. They went into the downstairs laboratory. Above their heads, they could hear footsteps, backwards and forwards above their heads.

"Once I heard it weeping," Poole said suddenly.

"Weeping?" asked Utterson. He felt chilled with terror.

"Weeping like a lost soul, a soul in torment," said Poole.

Poole took an axe from one of the crates. They put the candle down and crept up the stairs. They could still hear footsteps in the room.

"Jekyll! I demand to see you!" shouted Utterson.

"Utterson," said the voice, "for God's sake, have mercy!"

"That's not Jekyll's voice!" said Utterson, "break down the door!"

Poole swung the axe and broke the wooden door. A cry of a terrified animal came from the room. Then silence. Poole and Utterson ran into the study. On the floor lay the twitching body of a small man, wearing clothes much too big for him. He held a crushed glass tube in his hand.

"We have come too late," said Utterson. "This is Mr Hyde. And he is dead. Now we must find your master."

He and Poole searched everywhere for Dr Jekyll, but there was no sign of him. At last, they found an envelope

on his desk, addressed in Jekyll's handwriting to Mr Utterson. The lawyer opened it and took out a short note.

"Today's date," said the lawyer, "so Jekyll was in his house today! Where is he now? And why has he fled from us?"

"What does my master say?" asked Poole.

"MY DEAR UTTERSON," read Utterson. *"When this falls into your hands, I shall have disappeared. Death is near for me. Go and read the letter which Lanyon told me he had written to you before his death. Then, if you want to hear more, turn to the confession of*

Your unworthy and unhappy friend

HENRY JEKYLL"

"Here it is," said Poole, handing a thick envelope to the lawyer.

"I shall go home and do as Jekyll tells me," said Mr Utterson. "I shall come back here at midnight, Poole. Then we shall call the police. I pray to God that this terrible mystery will soon be explained."

CHAPTER NINE

A letter from Dr Lanyon

Mr Utterson sighed as he sat down in his study. It was now ten o'clock on that terrible evening. First, he opened Dr Lanyon's letter.

"TO J. UTTERSON

On the 10 December, I was surprised to receive a letter from Henry Jekyll. He begged me to help him that night. I was to go to his house and bring the fourth drawer from the top of his cabinet, with all its contents, back to my consulting rooms. At midnight, I was to admit a man who would come on Jekyll's behalf and give him the drawer. The letter ended strangely, saying that if I did not do this, I would have seen the last of Henry Jekyll.

Of course, I thought the man was mad. But I felt I should do as he asked. I did bring the drawer back to my rooms. I examined the contents very carefully – there were white powders wrapped in paper, an evil-smelling red liquid in a test tube, and other ingredients which I did not recognise.

I read some pages of a notebook in the drawer. There were dates and comments such as "Total failure!" which seemed so strange that I loaded my revolver just before midnight. Then I waited. At midnight exactly, someone knocked gently on my door. I opened it. A small man crouched against the pillars.

"Have you come from Dr Jekyll?" I asked.

The man nodded, glanced behind him and came in. I could see him more clearly now. He had a terrible expression on his face. His clothes were much too big for him; but I could not laugh. He was revolting, abnormal. He seemed impatient and over-excited.

"Have you got it?" he cried. "Have you got it?"

He came up to me and shook my arm in his desperation. My blood ran cold and I removed his hand from my arm.

"Sit down, sir," I told him, sitting myself in the hope that he would copy me. I felt nothing but horror at the sight of this strange creature.

"Forgive my impatience, sir, "he said quietly. "I have come on behalf of your colleague, Dr Henry Jekyll. I understand..."

He paused and put his hand to his throat. He seemed on the point of hysteria. "I understand...a drawer..."

I took pity on him. I pointed to the drawer on the floor. The creature sprang into action, then stopped and laid his hand upon his heart. He started to grind his teeth and his face was terrible to see. I was terrified. I thought he might become mad, or die, at any moment.

"Be calm," I told him.

He gave a dreadful smile and tore the
sheet away from the drawer. At the sight
of its contents, he gave a sob of relief, so
loud that I was petrified.

"Have you a measuring glass?" he asked,
trying to control his voice.

I handed him one.

"Thank you," he said, and he smiled. He began to measure
out the red liquid, then added one of the powders. As the
crystals melted, the liquid began to lighten in colour and
bubble and give off a strong smell. Suddenly, the bubbling
stopped, and the glass was full of a dark green liquid.

"Now," said the visitor, "will you allow me to leave your
house with this glass, and ask me no questions? Or are you so
curious that you wish to see what happens? Think carefully
before you answer! I shall do as you decide. Remember, you
can choose to be none the wiser, or you can enter a whole
new area of knowledge."

I tried to remain calm.

"Sir," I said, "you do not make any sense. But I have now
gone too far. I must see this to the end."

"Remember, Lanyon," said my visitor. "What follows is
under the vows of our profession as doctors. Your views have
always been too narrow. You have always said that medicine
cannot....watch!"

He put the glass to his lips and drank. He gave a loud cry.

He reeled, and staggered, clutched at the table, held on, gasped for breath with his mouth wide open. His eyes bulged and stared. His whole body seemed to swell. His face became black, his features melting and changing.

I leapt to my feet, ran back to the wall and put my arms up in front of me so that I could not see this...my mind was filled with terror. I looked again. There in front of me – pale and trembling and stumbling – was Henry Jekyll.

"My God!" I screamed. "O God! My God! O God!"

That is what happened that terrible December night. Still I ask myself if I believe it, and I cannot answer. My life is shaken to the roots. I cannot sleep. The most dreadful terror fills me night and day. I know that I am going to die.

Your friend

Dr Lanyon

Utterson put down the letter.

"My poor dear Jekyll," he sighed. "Why did you do it?"

He picked up the second letter with a heavy heart.

"Please God this letter will give me the answer."

CHAPTER TEN

A letter from Dr Jekyll

My dear Utterson

This is the last time that I, Henry Jekyll, can think my own thoughts. I write to you now before it is too late.

As I grew up, I soon discovered that man is made up of good and evil. One day, I had an amazing thought. What if the good and the evil in us could each lead a separate life! How much pleasanter life would be! The bad one would go his own way and leave his good twin to lead his own life free from the fear of evil.

I worked to find a way of putting my ideas into practice through the use of certain medicines. I would change myself into a separate person who would be the evil part of me. I knew that my work was dangerous. I knew that I could die. But I had to go on with it. I discovered the last ingredient that I needed, and bought a large quantity of it. There was no going back for me now.

One night, I took this medicine for the first time. Immediately, pain ran through my body. My bones creaked and hurt and I felt sick. Then afterwards, when these symptoms had gone, I felt different – lighter, younger and...dare I say it?... I felt evil.

I looked at my new self in my mirror. I decided to call

him Edward Hyde. However, I did notice how small and sickly Hyde was compared to the good Jekyll he had replaced. I was not repelled by Hyde as other people were later on. They recognised that he was evil and were afraid. I saw his evil and I was pleased. Then I took another sip of the medicine and I changed back into Henry Jekyll, the respectable doctor.

But something happened that I did not expect. I soon became a slave to my evil self. I wanted to be Hyde more and more. So I rented a furnished house for him, and a housekeeper. I told my servants to make Hyde welcome should he visit me. I even drew up my Will with you, dear friend, in case I should disappear.

Other men have often hired murderers and thieves to carry out their evil crimes. But I did these things for pleasure. I went out night after night to drink and take pleasure in harming my fellow men. As Mr Hyde, I had no conscience. As Dr Jekyll, I had sometimes to put right Hyde's wrongs.

One morning, I woke up and saw that terrible hand on my bed-clothes – the thick, hairy hand of Hyde. How could this have happened? I had not taken any medicine! I looked at Hyde in the mirror and saw that he had grown taller. I quickly swallowed the medicine that I always kept ready and went down to breakfast as Dr Jekyll. I could hardly eat. That day, I decided to give up Hyde. I was afraid that I, Henry Jekyll, might disappear for ever. But I did not give up Hyde's house, or throw away the medicine; but I tried hard for two months to ignore him.

But soon I was tortured with a longing to be Hyde again. Once more, in a moment of weakness, I drank the medicine. My devil had been caged too long and he came out roaring. That night, I met an old gentleman on a footpath. He stopped to talk and I hit him with my stick. I delighted in every blow. Evil raged throughout my body.

As Henry Jekyll, I wept for what I had done and prayed to God to forgive me. Once more, I decided to give up Edward Hyde. One fine January day, I sat in the park listening to the birds singing. I was full of goodwill towards my fellow men. My friends had recently been to dine. I was happy. Suddenly, I felt sick and faint. My thoughts became dark and gloomy. I looked down in horror. My clothes were too big for my shrunken body. The hand that lay on my knee was thick-skinned and hairy. Yet I had not drunk any medicine.

I was Edward Hyde, a wanted murderer!

I could still think clearly. I knew that if I returned home for my medicine, I might be arrested. I remembered one thing in my terror. My handwriting had remained the same. I wrote to Dr Lanyon, asking him to meet me with more medicine. He has told you in his letter what happened that terrible night. Poor Lanyon! How I hated to see the horror on his face!

It was then, for the first time, that I feared Edward Hyde.

The worst time of my life came in the days that followed. I

had to take stronger and stronger medicine to keep Hyde away. If I fell asleep for a few seconds in my chair, I woke up as him. As Hyde became stronger, so Jekyll weakened. We began to hate each other. He fears me. He knew that I could kill him at any moment by killing myself.

I shall say little more, except that my life as Dr Jekyll became a torment. Soon, I faced another problem. The salt that I needed for my potion was running out and I could not buy one of the same strength.

I must seal this letter now, while I have the time. If I should change into Hyde as I write it, he will tear it to pieces. Half an hour from now, I shall be that dreaded man for ever. What will happen to Hyde? Will he die for his crime, or find the courage to die at the last minute? I shall not know the answer; but I have heard you and Poole outside my door, and you will know the answer, my dear friend.

Now I put down my pen. This is the hour of my death.
Henry Jekyll

Mr Utterson put down the letter and stared into the fire.

"This is the most terrible story I have ever read," he cried to himself.

And he covered his face with his hands.

Glossary

Key:

adj	adjective
adv	adverb
n	noun
phr	phrase
phr v	phrasal verb
(superl)	superlative
vi	intransitive verb
vt	transitive verb

admit, to	*vt*	if you admit someone to a room, you allow them to enter the room	41
ash	*n*	what is left after paper or wood has been burnt	21
be rewarded, to	*passive*	if you are rewarded for something, something positive happens as a result of it	14
blackmail	*n*	threatening to harm someone, unless they do as you tell them or pay you money	7
bow, to	*vi*	to bend your body when greeting someone	17
bulge, to	*vi*	to stick out	44
butler	*n*	the most important of the male servants in a house	29

chill someone to the bone, to	*phr*	to make someone feel very frightened or anxious	28
clench, to	*vt*	to shut tightly	24
clerk	*phr*	a person who works in an office, doing administrative tasks	24
consulting rooms	*phr*	the room where a doctor sees his/her patients	41
cool	*adj*	not worried or troubled	8
deformed	*adj*	if something is deformed, it doesn't have the usual shape	11
dingy	*adj*	shabby and a bit depressing	20
disgrace	*n*	something that is shocking or unacceptable	12
dissect, to	*vt*	to cut up carefully	22
eerie	*adj*	strange and frightening	34
fall into someone's hands, to	*phr*	if something falls into your hands, it comes into your possession	40
feverish	*adj*	with a high temperature and unwell	23
flickering	*adj*	unsteady; blowing	34
foot of the stairs, the	*phr*	the bottom of the stairs	34
forge, to	*vt*	if you forge a signature, you copy it and use it illegally	25

foul play	*phr*	criminal or violent behaviour	32
give someone your word of honour, to	*phr*	if you give someone your word of honour, you mean that you are telling them the truth	23
haunt, to	*vt*	to go regularly to a place	13
have mercy!	*phr*	have pity on me! do not harm me!	38
hearth	*n*	the floor of a fireplace, where you build the fire itself	33
hint at, to	*phr*	to make subtle remarks about something	28
hoarse	*adj*	rough-sounding	35
housekeeper	*n*	a person who looks after a house for its owner and manages any servants	46
huddled	*adj*	sitting very close together	20
husky	*adj*	slightly rough	15
hysteria	*n*	a state of having very strong, uncontrolled feelings	42
ill-feeling	*phr*	bad feeling; dislike	25
knocker	*n*	a kind of metal handle attached to a door, used to knock on the door	8
last will and testament	*phr*	the document that gives details of who you are leaving your money and possessions to when you die	12
littered with boxes	*phr*	with lots of boxes, all over the place	22

low in spirits	*phr*	depressed	31
master	*n*	if you are a servant, your master is the man you work for	19
murky	*adj*	dark and unpleasant	20
neglected	*adj*	not looked after or cared for	8
nerve: his nerve almost gave way	*phr*	if someone's nerve gives way, they lose their calm and begin to panic	34
on behalf of...	*phr*	in the place of...	41
petrified	*adj*	extremely frightened; unable to move	43
put your ideas into practice, to	*phr*	to start to act according to you ideas	45
reel, to	*vi*	to move unsteadily, as though you are going to fall	44
relief	*n*	the feeling you have when you realise that you no longer need to worry about something	43
repel, to	*vt*	to disgust	29
safe	*n*	a very strong metal box to keep important documents or valuable things in	12
sake: for your sake	*phr*	if you hope something for someone's sake, you mean you hope that this is the case because otherwise the person will have problems	23

Scotland Yard	*n*	the main police station in London	20
shrink away from, to	*phr*	to move backwards, away from something or someone, because you are frightened or don't want to be seen	15
sneer	*n*	an expression of contempt, which shows you have a lack of respect	8
snort, to	*vi*	to make a loud noise in your nose when you breathe; to say something with a sneer	16
sourly	*adv*	in a bad-tempered way, or in a way that shows you disapprove	21
stagger, to	*vi*	to walk very unsteadily	44
step into someone's shoes, to	*phr*	to take someone's place	12
stroke	*n*	a serious medical condition in which there is bleeding in the brain, causing paralysis and problems with speech	37
trample over, to	*phr*	to step heavily on something	7
twitching	*adj*	making sudden little nervous movements	38
vow	*n*	a promise	43
walking-cane	*n*	a walking stick	9
wanted	*adj*	if a person is wanted, the police are looking for them	47
wretched	*adj*	poor and unpleasant	8

Dr Jekyll & Mr Hyde
Test Yourself

Exercise 1

Are these sentences true (T) or false (F)?

1   Mr Enfield saw a girl run into a little man and fall over.

2   Mr Enfield ran after Mr Hyde, and took him back to where the girl was.

3   Mr Utterson, a well-known police officer, was Mr Enfield's friend.

4   Mr Utterson didn't like Dr Jekyll's will, because in it the doctor would give what he had to Mr Enfield after he died.

5   Dr Lanyon told Mr Utterson that Dr Jekyll had begun to go wrong ten years before.

6   Sir Carew and Hyde met in a street and Carew hit Hyde with his walking-cane, so Hyde knocked him to the ground.

7   A maid saw the murder from her window, and she recognised the attacker was Mr Hyde.

8   Mr Utterson received a letter from Mr Hyde, in which Mr Hyde threatened to kill him.

9   Mr Guest, Mr Utterson's head clerk, said the handwriting on the letter and on the invitation were the same.

10   Before Dr Lanyon died, he had left a letter for Dr Jekyll.

Exercise 2

Can you answer these questions?

1   Who saw Dr Jekyll sitting by his window?

2   Why does Dr Jekyll say he can't invite his friends up to his room?

3   Who is Poole?

4   Who was sitting round the fire at Jekyll's house?

5   Why were Poole and Utterson worried about Jekyll's voice?

6   Whose body did Poole and Utterson find in Jekyll's room?

7   What did Lanyon find inside Jekyll's drawer?

8   What happened to the strange small man when he took the medicine at Lanyon's house?

9   Why did Mr Hyde carry out evil crimes?

10   Why did Mr Hyde fear Dr Jekyll?

Answers

Exercise 1	1 F; 2 T; 3 F; 4 F; 5 T; 6 F; 7 T; 8 F; 9 T; 10 F

Exercise 2

1 Mr Utterson and Mr Enfield
2 because the place is untidy
3 Dr Jekyll's butler
4 Dr Jekyll's servants'
5 because it had changed
6 Mr Hyde's
7 there were some white powders wrapped in paper, an evil-smelling red liquid and some other ingredients
8 he turned into Dr Jekyll
9 for pleasure
10 because by killing himself, Dr Jekyll could kill Mr Hyde